The
Christmas
Crocodile

The Christmas Crocodile

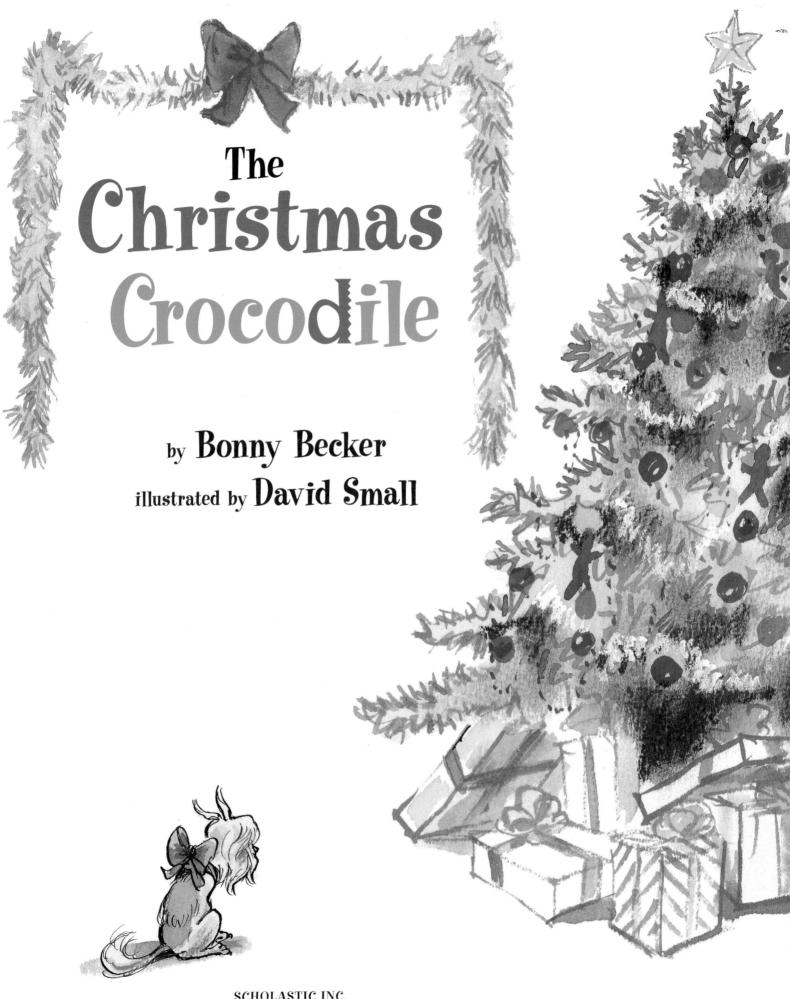

The
Christmas
Crocodile

by **Bonny Becker**

illustrated by **David Small**

SCHOLASTIC INC.

New York Toronto London Auckland Sydney
Mexico City New Delhi Hong Kong

ISBN 0-439-10481-5

Text copyright © 1998 by Bonny Becker.
Illustrations copyright © 1998 by David Small.
All rights reserved. Published by Scholastic Inc., 555 Broadway,
New York, NY 10012, by arrangement with Simon & Schuster Books
for Young Readers, Simon & Schuster Children's Publishing Division.
SCHOLASTIC and associated logos are trademarks and/or registered
trademarks of Scholastic Inc.

12 11 10 9 8 7 6 5 4 3 2 1   9/9 0 1 2 3 4/0

Printed in the U.S.A.   08

First Scholastic printing, November 1999

The Christmas Crocodile didn't mean to be bad, not really.
Alice Jayne found him on Christmas Eve under the tree. He wore a
red bow around his neck. It was lovely. Except he ate it.

Then he ate a couple of presents, just little ones, and he gnawed on Father's shoe, ate the wreath in the hall, and ran away with the Christmas roast—a big one. He was eating up Christmas and no one knew what to do with him.

"Send the beast to Africa," huffed Uncle Theodore, who had once hunted wild game there.

"He must be put in an orphanage," fretted Aunt Figgy, who worried a lot, especially about orphans.

"Lock him in the back room, Alice Jayne," instructed Father, "while we consider the situation."

"Better give him the pumpkin pie," said Mother. "He still looks hungry."

Alice Jayne crossed her arms and tapped her toe while the Christmas Crocodile slunk into the back room. She closed and locked the door with a firm click.

But then she thought she heard him sniffling in there. Not feeling hungry after all, she slipped him the pineapple upside-down cake, along with the pie.

"We could make him into a pair of shoes," said Uncle Theodore, who was busy considering things back in the parlor.

"Or a pet for some orphans," said Aunt Figgy.

"I wonder whose presents he ate?" said Cousin Elwood, who had finally finished eating all the fudge the Crocodile had missed and could now speak.

"He's nice," said Alice Jayne. "Maybe we could keep him."

"Unheard of!" protested
Aunt Figgy.

"But it's Christmas!" said Alice Jayne.

"Irrelevant," harrumphed Uncle
Theodore.

"He's just a little hungry, that's
all," said Alice Jayne.

"Perhaps the zoo would take him,"
said Father, worriedly.

"He needs a real home!" cried Alice Jayne.

"We'll think about it, dear," said
Mother, and she sent them all to bed.

The Christmas Crocodile didn't mean to be bad, not really. But in the middle of the night he ate through the back room door, swallowed twenty-nine crumpets on the kitchen counter, a box of pralines, one fruitcake, five golden oranges, the left stove-top burner, and a plate of ginger star cookies—they were for Santa!

Then he crept upstairs. One door was open just a bit. He nuzzled it open a bit more. Inside, he found tasty talcum powder, a feather boa that tickled his tongue, and a swig of perfume. Just right! Then he found ten pink toes. He sniffed them. Hmmmmm. He licked them. Yummmmm. He took a teeny, tiny bite.

Aunt Figgy's scream shivered cobwebs in the attic, and made the dust dance on a bottle of wine in the cellar.

"I'll save you!" roared Uncle Theodore, waking with a start from a dream about cannibals.

"Run for your lives!" shrieked Cousin Elwood.

"There's blood!" gasped Aunt Figgy, pointing to a pinprick of red on her little toe.

"Where is he?" sighed Mother.

The Christmas Crocodile didn't mean to be bad, not really.
They found him hiding under Alice Jayne's bed. He tried to wag
his tail in a friendly fashion, but it was too cramped.
"Into the cellar with him!" commanded Father.

The Christmas Crocodile scooted sadly down the stairs to the basement. He shivered in the cold, but Alice Jayne crossed her arms and tapped her toe. She closed and locked the door with a firm click.

She went back to bed and lay under her warm blanket. She swallowed a lump in her throat.

Somehow it didn't feel like the night before Christmas anymore.

She slipped out of bed, her blanket held close, and crept quietly
down the stairs to the basement.

She wrapped the Crocodile snugly, tucking her blanket under his
chin. She found an old candy cane, covered with lint, in her
bathrobe pocket. She broke it in two.

"One for me and one for you," she whispered.

The Christmas Crocodile gulped happily and closed his eyes.

The cellar door creaked open.

"You know, he could be an *orphan*," hissed Aunt Figgy, slipping inside. She tucked her hot water bottle under the Crocodile's toes.

"A crocodile saved my life once," announced Uncle Theodore, coming in behind Aunt Figgy. "Decent chap, really." He spread his Zulu robe over the Crocodile's tail.

"Perhaps he's learned his lesson," said Father, peering around the door and holding up his red earmuffs.

"Is it time to open the presents yet?" yawned Cousin Elwood, stumbling in. He patted the Crocodile on the snout and fell asleep.

Mother came last. She spread a fluffy comforter across them all.
"We couldn't leave him alone," she said. "Not on Christmas Eve."
Everyone nodded.
The Christmas Crocodile let out a contented snore.
"Full at last," observed Father.
Everyone sighed.
Then they all settled down to wait . . .
. . . and watch.

The Christmas Crocodile didn't mean to be bad, not really. But somehow everyone fell asleep. Somehow the Crocodile slipped away. Somehow he ate through the basement door.

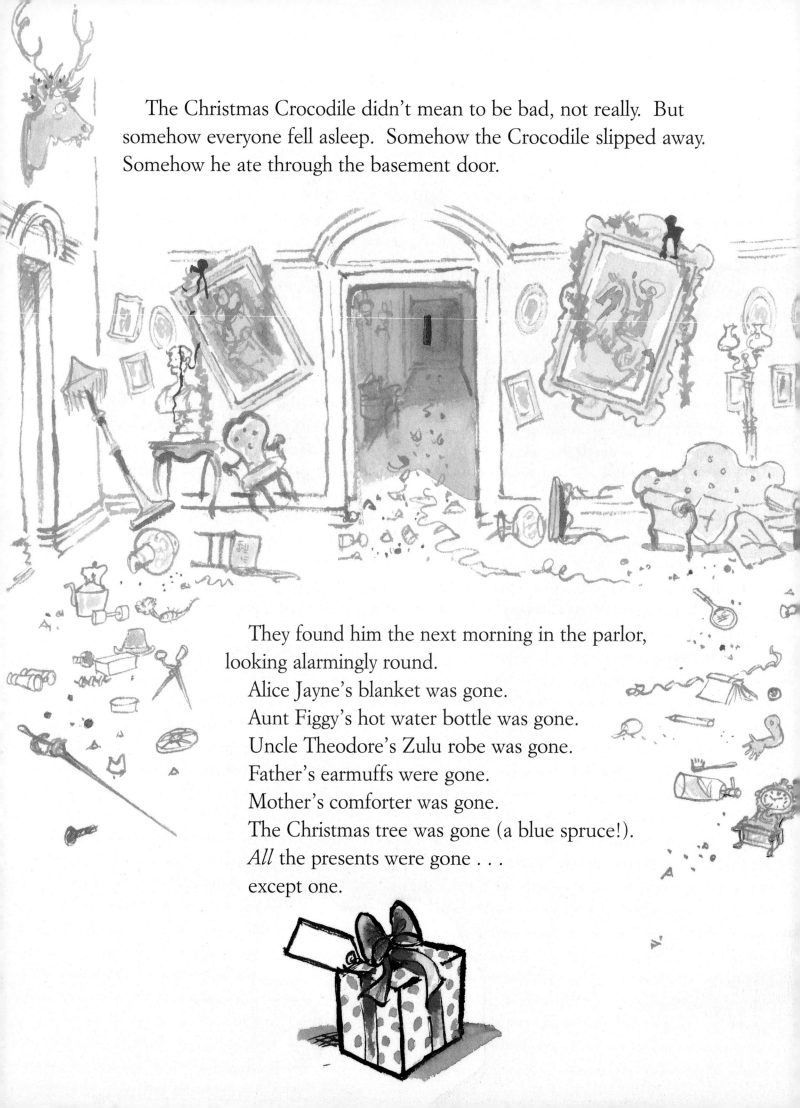

They found him the next morning in the parlor, looking alarmingly round.

Alice Jayne's blanket was gone.

Aunt Figgy's hot water bottle was gone.

Uncle Theodore's Zulu robe was gone.

Father's earmuffs were gone.

Mother's comforter was gone.

The Christmas tree was gone (a blue spruce!).

All the presents were gone . . .

except one.

"Pump his stomach!" yowled Elwood.
"Send for my elephant gun!" roared Uncle Theodore.
"Those were for the orphans!" shrieked Aunt Figgy
about the missing presents.

"What's that?" asked Alice Jayne, pointing at the one small present remaining.

"If *he* didn't want it, it must be bad," Cousin Elwood announced.

"Quite so," agreed Uncle Theodore. Aunt Figgy nodded.

"I'll open it," said Alice Jayne, and she quickly tore off the ribbon.

Dec. 25
Dear Family:
Hope you like Crocodiles !!!
Love,
Uncle Carbuncle
xxxooo

"It's from Uncle Carbuncle!"
cried Cousin Elwood.

"Good old Carbuncle," shouted
Uncle Theodore.

"Carbuncle, at last," breathed Aunt Figgy.

"But we haven't got an Uncle Carbuncle,"
protested Alice Jayne.

Since she was right, no one knew what
to say. But Alice Jayne knew. It meant
that the Christmas Crocodile had been
delivered to the wrong address.

And sure enough, the doorbell rang.

At the door were two deliverymen.

"Take him away," Father said, firmly.

The two men hoisted up the Crocodile and staggered down the snowy steps to a waiting van.

"Good-bye," said Alice Jayne, sadly.

The Christmas Crocodile snuffled. One great crocodile tear ran down his snout. But then he saw the sign on the delivery van.

"I'll come visit soon," promised Alice Jayne as they loaded him into the van.

"Merry Christmas!" cried the deliverymen.

"Merry Christmas!" cried one and all.

The Christmas Crocodile didn't mean to be bad, not really. He waved his tail farewell, but, as the van rounded the corner, it did look rather like a deliveryman's cap in his jaws.

"Well," sighed Mother, "peace at last."
"Yes," agreed everyone . . .
. . . except Alice Jayne, who didn't say a word.